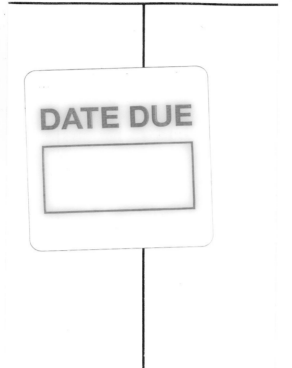

A Horse and A Hound

A Goat and A Gander

ALICE AND MARTIN PROVENSEN

ATHENEUM   1980   NEW YORK

To Karen, Dacie, Allelu and Cheryl

by the same authors

THE YEAR AT MAPLE HILL FARM

Library of Congress Cataloging in Publication Data

Provensen, Alice.
  A horse and a hound, a goat and a gander.

  SUMMARY: Four farm animals, each with a distinct and
highly idiosyncratic personality, liven the days at
Maple Hill Farm.
  [1. Domestic animals—Fiction] I. Provensen, Martin,
joint author. II. Title.
  PZ7.P9457Ho   [E]   80-13259

ISBN 0-689-30793-4

Copyright © 1979 by Alice and Martin Provensen
All rights reserved
Printed by A. Hoen & Company, Baltimore, Maryland
Bound by A. Horowitz & Sons/ Bookbinders
Fairfield, New Jersey
First American Edition

MAPLE HILL FARM is a very special place in the country. It is reached by a rough dirt road. At the end of a long lane is a white house that needs painting and a grey barn with a tin roof that leaks. Grass grows here that always needs mowing. It is enclosed by a fence that always needs mending.

Sometimes the sun shines on this special place. Sometimes the rain falls and everything is muddy. In winter it snows and the pond freezes over and the electricity fails – but these are not the things that make Maple Hill Farm so special. What makes it special are the very special animals that belong to the farm.

There are fancy little chickens living on the farm and some plain brown hens.
There is a big black dog and a little black dog and a new brown hound on the farm.
There are more or less cats, depending on the time of year,
and there are a few sheep, a few cows, a few geese and some goats.

There are several horses living on the farm. Some have been bought for the farm, some are boarding at the farm and once in a while a horse is given to Maple Hill simply because he needs a home. Most gift horses are already named when you get them and their names can be something of a mystery.

BASHFUL BOY is a horse who found a home at Maple Hill Farm. He is the colour of burnt toast. He can't eat hay, it makes him cough. He can't sleep on straw, it makes him sneeze.

He needs special feed and special bedding but he is worth the trouble. He is quiet so no one is afraid of him. He is polite so he makes friends easily. BASHFUL is a gentleman.

BASHFUL isn't the least bit shy out riding.
He has never refused a fence no matter how high. BASHFUL is bold.

The trouble with BASHFUL is he just doesn't want to go anywhere if he can't get there
on his own four feet. He dislikes strangers.

BASHFUL isn't the least bit timid in the pasture.
He fends off stray dogs in the winter and the sheep trust him. BASHFUL is brave.

He hates crowds. He detests horse shows. Do you suppose BASHFUL BOY is bashful?

Oh well, most animals would rather be safe
at home with their friends.

One of BASHFUL's special friends
is a great big brown bloodhound named JOHN.

JOHN is the colour of burnt toast, too. His skin is too big for his bones.
He looks old and sad, but really JOHN is young and playful and gentle as a kitten.
He might knock you down when he wags his tail but he would never hurt anyone.
One of the most important things about JOHN is his nose.

JOHN, THE HUNTER, has a beautiful nose.

When JOHN is not sleeping ...   he is usually out hunting with his nose.

JOHN doesn't have to see where something is, he can smell where it is.

JOHN brings home the things he finds. He carries them in his mouth.

JOHN carries baby rabbits as gently as a mother cat carries kittens.

JOHN, THE RETRIEVER, finds all sorts of things and brings them home.

He finds old shoes ...   and more old shoes ...   and more old shoes.

Where do you suppose he finds all these awful old shoes he loves so?

GREEDY JOHN loves cakes and biscuits.

He can scent a cake baking in the oven.

He can scent a biscuit cooling on a plate.

JOHN is not allowed to steal from the table, but the temptation is great.

JOHN can resist temptation, but only if he hears someone coming.

Then he pretends it's not the biscuits that interest him.

JOHN is clever, but somehow he can never fool anyone.

But you can't fool JOHN either. You can never hide from JOHN, THE TRACKER.

JOHN doesn't have to see you, he can trail you everywhere you've been. JOHN would never let you be lost for long. He will lead you back home and take you into the house.

Most dogs like to be in the house … especially if it is cold and rainy and the kitchen is warm and smells of baking bread and tea is nearly ready. JOHN likes people and cooking and he will come into the house now and then to be sociable, but he never stays very long.

JOHN likes the barn. He can come and go as he pleases. The horses' stalls are warm on cold and rainy nights. The hay smells good and there is lots of room for everybody. JOHN likes the cows and goats, too. They smell sweet and they are nice and quiet.

Except for billy goats who butt and rams who can be rambunctious and bulls
who stamp and snort and can be rude, most hooved animals are gentle and have nice manners.
Goats and sheep in particular are quiet and courteous and there is nothing so pretty
as a polite white goat.

GOAT DEAR is the nicest nanny goat of all.
She is allowed to run loose. Well, it's not exactly that she is allowed to run loose …
it's just that it's impossible to confine her. You can't enclose her behind a fence.

GOAT DEAR can jump over any fence.
Then she eats the bark from trees.

You tether her in a place where she
can't damage anything but a few weeds.

In no time at all she is hopelessly tangled
in her tie rope and has to be unsnarled.

Then she runs off to see what there is
to eat in the way of trees and flowers.

Oh well, Maple Hill Farm probably has enough trees and flowers to spare and it's somehow worth it to see her free. GOAT DEAR will go for a walk with you just like a dog.

If she gets tired of following along, she will turn back and find her way to the house and wait for you there. Sometimes GOAT DEAR finds her way into the house.

GOAT DEAR is not exactly housebroken but it's fun to see her indoors.

She is not nervous or ill at ease but looks at everything with curiosity.

What do you suppose "indoors" looks like to a goat?

It can't be very interesting, GOAT DEAR never stays very long.

GOAT DEAR would rather be
in the barnyard where there is more excitement.
There is a speckled rooster crowing in the barnyard.
There is a good old little red hen looking after
baby chicks in the barnyard.

And there is a whole big hissing, honking gaggle of geese in the barnyard.
The biggest, crankiest, honkiest goose is a gander named EVIL MURDOCH.

Even as a gosling ...

EVIL gave promise of a remarkably bad temper.

As he grew, his manners got no better, nor did his disposition.

Now that he is fully grown, EVIL is a noisy bully.
He stretches and stamps and glowers at strangers.
He casts angry glances at planes overhead.
He rushes the horses and pulls their tails ...

sometimes getting a free ride!

Sometimes in the spring, when he is particularly difficult, EVIL has to be penned up and even then he tries to hammer your shins through the fence when you are feeding him.

But once in a while, if you are not afraid, you can pick him up and hold him close and smooth his feathers. Then he will make soft noises and put his head under your arm. EVIL MURDOCH is sentimental.

EVIL is silly and sentimental, if you can use such words about a bird. He is always falling in love.

He falls in love with old wagon wheels and broken barrels and sometimes even stones.
He will sit near them and rub his head against them and smooth the earth around them …
until some other object catches his attention. Now he is in love with hub caps.

He loves a hub cap on the farm truck. He sits near it and rubs his head against it and smooths
the earth around it. When the farm truck is driven away, EVIL is left, crankier than ever,

waiting for another shiny hub cap to roll into the drive.

Unfortunately, truck wheels are dangerous,
and not every truck driver realizes they are objects of affection.
EVIL is bumped often enough. This time he is hurt.

The geese worry around him and wait with him.
Making small noises, EVIL allows himself to be caught and carried to the car.

Surprisingly enough, EVIL, who has never been in a car before, is calm on the way to the vet's. He looks out of the window with curiosity.

Surprisingly enough, EVIL, who has never been to the vet's before, is dignified. He allows the doctor to mend his beautiful wing.

It is no surprise at all that EVIL MURDOCH, tired as he is, gives everyone a mean pinch when he gets back to the barnyard. It just shows he's glad to be home again.

But then, almost all animals are happy to be safe at home with their special friends.